WAGON WHEELS

WAGON WHEELS

Story by Barbara Brenner
Pictures by Don Bolognese

HarperTrophy

A Division of HarperCollins*Publishers*

Wagon Wheels
Text copyright © 1978 by Barbara Brenner
Illustrations copyright © 1978, 1993 by Don Bolognese
Printed in the U.S.A. All rights reserved.
❖

Library of Congress Cataloging-in-Publication Data
Brenner, Barbara.
    Wagon wheels / by Barbara Brenner ; pictures by Don Bolognese.
        p.   cm. — (An I can read book)
    Summary: Shortly after the Civil War a black family travels to Kansas to
take advantage of the free land offered through the Homestead Act.
    ISBN 0-06-020668-3. — ISBN 0-06-020669-1 (lib. bdg.)
    ISBN 0-06-444052-4 (pbk.)
    [1. Frontier and pioneer life—Kansas—Fiction.   2. Kansas—Fiction.   3.
Afro-Americans—Fiction.]   I. Bolognese, Don, ill.   II. Title.   III. Series.
[PZ7.B7518Wag   1993]   92-18780
[E]—dc20   CIP
                                                                              AC

Newly Illustrated edition.
New Harper Trophy edition, 1993.

· CONTENTS ·

Chapter I • THE DUGOUT

"There it is, boys," Daddy said.

"Across this river

is Nicodemus, Kansas. That is where

we are going to build our house.

There is free land

for everyone here in the West.

All we have to do is go and get it."

We had come a long way

to get to Kansas.

All the way from Kentucky.

It had been a hard trip,

and a sad one.

Mama died on the way.

Now there were just the four of us—

Daddy, Willie, Little Brother, and me.

"Come on, boys," Daddy called.

"Let's put our feet on free dirt."

We crossed the river, wagon and all.

A man was waiting for us

on the other side.

"I am Sam Hickman," he said.

"Welcome to the town of Nicodemus."

"Why, thank you, Brother,"

Daddy said.

"But where *is* your town?"

"Right here," Mr. Hickman said.

We did not see any houses.

But we saw smoke

coming out of holes in the prairie.

"Shucks!" my daddy said.

"Holes in the ground

are for rabbits and snakes,

not for free black people.

I am a carpenter.

I can build fine wood houses

for this town."

"No time to build wood houses now,"

Mr. Hickman told my daddy.

"Winter is coming.

And winter in Kansas is *mean*.

Better get yourself a dugout

before the ground freezes."

Daddy knew Sam Hickman was right.

We got our shovels

and we dug us a dugout.

It wasn't much of a place—

dirt floor,

dirt walls,

no windows.

And the roof

was just grass and branches.

But we were glad

to have that dugout

when the wind began to whistle

across the prairie.

Every night Willie lit the lamp

and made a fire.

I cooked a rabbit stew

or fried a pan of fish

fresh from the river.

After supper

Daddy would always say,

"How about a song or two?"

He would take out his banjo and

Plink-a-plunk! Plink-a-plunk!

Pretty soon

that dugout felt like home.

Chapter II ⚫ INDIANS

Winter came.

And that Kansas winter *was* mean.

It snowed day after day.

We could not hunt or fish.

We had no more rabbit stew.

No more fish fresh from the river.

All we had was cornmeal mush to eat.

Then one day

there was no more cornmeal.

There was not a lick of food

in the whole town of Nicodemus.

And nothing left to burn for firewood.

Little Brother cried all the time—

he was so cold and hungry.

Daddy wrapped blankets around him.

"Hush, baby son," he said to him.

"Try to sleep.

Supply train will be coming soon."

But the supply train did not come.

Not that day or the next.

On the third day

we heard the sound of horses.

Daddy looked out to see who it was.

"Oh Lord!" he said.

"Indians!"

We were *so* scared.

We had all heard stories about Indians.

I tried to be brave.

"I will get my gun, Daddy," I said.

But Daddy said,

"Hold on, Johnny.

Wait and see what they do."

We watched from the dugout.

Everyone in Nicodemus

was watching the Indians.

First they made a circle.

Then each Indian

took something from his saddlebag

and dropped it on the ground.
The Indians turned and rode
straight toward the dugouts.
"Now they are coming for us!"
Willie cried.

We raised our guns.

But the Indians rode right past us

and kept on going.

We waited a long time

to be sure they were gone.

Then everyone ran out

into the snow to see

what the Indians had left.

It was FOOD!

Everyone talked at once.

"Look!"

"Fresh deer meat!"

"Fish!"

"Dried beans and squash!"

"And bundles of sticks

to keep our fires burning."

There was a feast

in Nicodemus that night.

But before we ate,

Daddy said to us,

"Johnny. Willie. Little Brother.

I want you to remember this day.

When someone says bad things

about Indians,

tell them the Osage Indians

saved our lives in Nicodemus."

Chapter III ◆ MOVING ON

When spring came, Daddy said,

"Boys, this prairie is too flat for me.

I want to find land

with trees and hills.

I'm going to move on."

I said, "I will start loading

the wagon."

But Daddy said, "Hold on, now.

I want you boys to stay.

You have shelter and friends here.

I will go alone.

I will send for you

when I find a place."

I was scared to stay alone.

So was Willie.

Poor Little Brother—

he tried to understand

what Daddy was saying.

We all listened as Daddy told us,

"I will leave you cornmeal

for your bread

and salt for your meat

and some molasses for a sweet.

You be good boys, you hear?

Take care of Little Brother.

Never let him out of your sight."

There were tears in Daddy's eyes

when he said good-bye to us.

Mrs. Sadler and Mrs. Hickman said,

"That Ed Muldie must be off his head

to leave you poor babies all alone."

I told them,

"I am no baby. I am eleven.

And Willie is eight.

We can take care of ourselves.

Little Brother is only three,

but we can take care of him, too."

We did what our daddy told us.

We hunted

and fished

and cooked

and swept the dugout clean.

We even baked our own corn bread.

And we never did let Little Brother
out of our sight.

We made him a wagon
out of an old box.

Mrs. Sadler gave us wheels for it.

We put Little Brother in the wagon,
and pulled him along with us.

You could hear the wheels squeak
a mile away.

When people in Nicodemus

heard that sound,

they always said,

"There go the Muldie boys."

One day we were picking
berries near the river.
Willie said, "Johnny, I smell smoke."
We looked up.

The whole sky was orange.

We heard someone shout,

"Prairie fire!"

We saw the fire behind us.

It was coming fast.

"We will be burned up," Willie cried.

"There is no place to run!"

I saw a deer

running toward the river.

"Quick!" I told Willie.

"Run to the river!"

We ran, pulling the wagon behind us.

People from Nicodemus

were running with us now.

When we got to the water,

I told Willie,

"Jump in. Hold the wagon.

I will hold Little Brother."

Everyone was jumping in around us.

Mr. Hickman helped me

hold Little Brother,

and Mr. Hill helped Willie
with the wagon.
There was fire and smoke all around,
but the water kept the fire from us.
We stayed there for a long time.
When the fire had died out,
we all walked home.

Chapter IV ◆ THE LETTER

April went by.

Then May and June.

We hunted and fished and waited

for a letter from Daddy.

Nothing came.

Then in July

the post rider came

with a letter for us.

It said:

Dear boys,

I have found fine free land

near Solomon City.

There is wood here to build a house,

and good black dirt

for growing corn and beans.

There is a map with this letter.

The map shows where I am

and where you are.

Follow the map.

Stay close to the Solomon River

until you come to the deer trail.

You will find me.

I know you can do it

because you are my fine big boys.

Love to you all, Daddy.

We started out the next day.

We piled corn bread and blankets

into Little Brother's wagon

until there was no room

for Little Brother.

"Can you walk like a big boy?"

I asked him. He nodded.

All of Nicodemus came out

to say good-bye—

the Hills, the Hickmans, the Sadlers....

They said,

"Poor babies.

Going a hundred fifty miles

all by themselves."

But we knew we could do it.

Our daddy had told us so.

We went to the river,

and we followed the map.

We walked all day.

When Little Brother got tired,

I carried him.

At night we stopped

and made a fire.

I told Willie,

"We will take turns.

First I will watch the fire

and you sleep.

Fire the gun sometimes.

It will scare wild animals away."

There were plenty of wild animals

on the prairie.

Wolves. Panthers. Coyotes.

Each night our fire and

the sound of the gun

kept them away.

But one night

I heard Willie call to me,

"Johnny, wake up. But don't move."

I opened my eyes.

There on the ground next to me

was a big prairie rattlesnake.

It was warming itself by the fire.

I didn't move.

I didn't *breathe,*

for fear it would bite me.

"What shall we do?" Willie whispered.

I tried to think what Daddy would do.

Then I remembered Daddy once told me

that snakes like warm places.

I said to Willie,

"Let the fire go out."

It seemed like *hours* we were there—

Willie, Little Brother, and me—

staying so still.

At last the fire went out.

The night air got chilly.

The snake moved away

into the darkness.

For twenty-two days

we followed the river.

Then one day

we came to a deer trail.

It led away from the river,

just like on the map.

"This way," I told my brothers.

We walked along the trail.

It led up a hill.

On the side of the hill

we saw a little house

with a garden in front.

We could see corn growing.

A man came out of the house.

When he saw us,

he began to run

toward us.

"Daddy!"

"Willie! Johnny! Little Brother!"

Then there was such hugging

and kissing

and talking

and crying

and laughing

and singing that ...

I bet they heard us all the way

back in Nicodemus!

And old Mrs. Sadler

must have said,

"Sounds like the Muldie boys

have found their daddy!"

Behind This Story . . .

Wagon Wheels is based on a true story. In 1878, Ed Muldie and his family left Kentucky to go to Kansas. They had heard about the Homestead Act, which promised free land to anyone who was willing to settle the West. The Muldies were among the thousands of black pioneers who left the South after the Civil War. Many of them, like the Muldies, settled in Kansas. The town of Nicodemus, which was named for a famous slave, was a black community.

The three boys in this story really did stay alone in a dugout. And they did travel one hundred fifty miles by themselves to find their father. The incident with the Osage Indians actually happened in the Nicodemus colony, and prairie fires were common in the whole Kansas territory.

The Muldie boys' story is documented in the memoirs of the late Lulu Sadler Craig, who came to Nicodemus as a child and spent much of her life teaching school and collecting information on the town's history. The material on which this book is based was used through a special arrangement with Craig Lively and the other members of Mrs. Craig's family.